❀ Created with Vellum

INVITATION TO MURDER

STEAMY COZY MYSTERY PREQUEL

MYSTERY, SHE WROTE

DELTA JAMES

Dedicated to My Two Best Friends:
Renee and Chris, without whom none of
what I do would be possible and to the Girls,
who bring joy to my life every single day

Acknowledgements As Always to My Team:
Development and Editing: Lori White,
Intuitive Editing and Development Services
Cover Design: Dar Albert, Wicked Smart Designs
Proofreader: Melinda Kaye Brandt

PROLOGUE

*W*hoever said life was a mystery to be lived and not a problem to be solved was only half right. Life should always be lived to the fullest but unsolved murders were most definitely both mysteries and problems to be solved.

FIONA

Mystery Readers of Maine Book Signing
Cabot Cove, Kennebunkport, Maine

God, it had been years since she'd been at a signing. Fiona Fowler loaded her hand truck with books and things for her table. She was late; she hadn't had coffee; and attending this signing was an incredibly bad idea. What the hell had she been thinking?

What the hell she was thinking was that she was going to lose a career she'd worked damn hard to create. There'd been a time when the world had been her oyster and she had made money hand-over-fist, but a nasty divorce and shattered self-esteem had robbed her of her natural self-confidence and her writing had suffered. It was time to get back into the real world and go back to work. All sitting on her laurels had done was to help her gain twenty pounds and run through what little money she'd managed to salvage from the destruction of her marriage.

Fiona hated making a fool of herself, and she was sure she was well on her way to doing just that. The Mystery Readers of Maine Book Signing was huge, as in more than one hundred and fifty authors and an expected attendance of over three thousand readers. She hadn't had a bestseller in years.

She snorted. Bestseller? She was barely keeping the roof over her head. There'd been a time she would have been welcomed at any signing—courted, even—but now she had to beg to grab up the table of an author that had canceled. She feared hearing whispers of 'what's she doing here?' It would be bad enough from other authors, but to hear it from readers would be like a knife through the heart.

In order to save money, she hadn't come yesterday and would only stay the one night. She managed to get everything into the event center and find the registration table for authors. A small woman with a pixie haircut and sharp eyes looked up at her.

"Can I help you?" she said in a tone that said she wasn't the least bit interested in helping anyone, much less a has-been. "Reader registration isn't for another four hours unless you're a VIP conference attendee."

"I'm Fiona Fowler. I'm one of the attending authors."

"Fowler?" the woman said, flipping through her registration materials. "Fowler… hmm, I don't see… oh, there you are. You're a last-minute addition and your name is penciled in. Let me see what I can do about an ID and lanyard."

"I'm running a little behind. Could I go ahead and start setting up my table?"

"I can't leave the registration desk and go traipsing about looking for you…"

"I wouldn't ask you to do that. Just let me get my table set up, and I'll come out and get them."

The woman took a deep breath, did a virtual eye roll, and sighed. "I suppose that will be all right. The table assignments are on the table just inside the doors by the continental breakfast. Yours should be easy to spot as it will be handwritten in red."

"Great. Thank you. I'll be out before the signing starts."

Fiona gathered the shattered bits of her self-confidence and wondered again why she had done this to herself. She had no one to blame as no one had invited her to the conference; she'd just heard a rumor about a last-minute cancellation and had called in a favor.

Stopping inside the entrance to the signing room, she found the table chart, and as promised the scheduled author's name had been marked out and her name had been scribbled in. It was misspelled, but it was there. It was in a back corner along the wall, which meant she'd have more room. Looking at the names of those closest to her, she groaned. Talk about sticking out like a sore thumb.

Two larger than normal tables were set side-by-side in the corner. They would be occupied by Christie Crofton, the retired Baltimore detective who had become an overnight sensation with her debut novel, *Prey for Us*. One book, and she was a featured author. The other diagonal table was held by Jessica Murdoch, a much revered and loved author with more than one hundred mystery and romantic suspense books to her name. She was the one they all looked to with stars in their eyes and envy in their hearts. Every book she wrote seemed to hit the top of every list known to mankind, and her most celebrated series was enjoying its sixth season on one of the streaming services.

Fiona would be sitting to Jessica's left. To Christie's right would be Lori Sykes, an up-and-coming author who had produced four books in three years, had won a prestigious award, and who was reputedly being courted by Fiona's old publisher—the same one who had dropped her like a hot stone when the third book in a row didn't perform to expectations.

She made her way to her table, reminding herself that she was here to try and bolster her failing sales and find new readers. So far none of those sitting closest to her were there. Good. Maybe she could get in and get set up and then slip out to get that name tag and something to eat. And coffee. Oh, how she needed her coffee.

Sliding behind her table, she pulled out her kit and began wrestling with her retractable banner. It seemed that all the authors had them these days. Fiona had asked the cover designer of her new book if she'd design a new logo so Fiona could rebrand herself. Jill had done an excellent job, and Fiona loved her new banner, table runner, business cards and swag items.

Standing in front of her table, Fiona smiled. Damn, it looked good, and she looked like she belonged. She wasn't sure she did, but at least she looked the part. No one had to know how carefully she had selected her outfit from several vintage clothing stores in the region. She looked quirky, but chic. She headed out to registration, waiting in line to retrieve her name badge.

"Name?" the woman asked, looking right at her.

"Fiona Fowler."

"Hmm… let me see."

"Earlier you found it written in."

"Oh right, the late comer. Well, let me see what I can do," the registration lady said, starting to hand-write a name tag.

Feeling humiliated, Fiona smiled as she waited and then took the hastily created name badge.

"Not happening," said the woman behind her.

"Fiona paid her money just like everyone else. I'm pretty damn sure that other box will have her proper name badge and lanyard."

The registration lady blinked several times, as did Fiona. She immediately recognized the woman from the back of her book and all of the morning shows. The woman had taken the media world by storm.

"Stella, see what you can do about finding Fiona's badge." There was no way that tone could be interpreted as anything other than an order and Stella quickly started searching through her boxes. In a matter of moments, she retrieved the nicely printed badge that resembled all the others.

Stella handed Fiona her badge as well as a badge for the woman who had come to her rescue—Christie Crofton.

"Come on, Fiona, you're sitting over with Jess and me. We've got Lori sitting with us, as well. This should be so much fun. I was so glad to see you were here and would be sitting with us. I absolutely love your books."

"You do?" asked Fiona as she let herself be led away.

"I absolutely do. I've read everything you've written. When I retired from Baltimore PD, I asked myself what I wanted to do, and decided I was going to pursue a lifelong dream. You're my inspiration."

"I am?" Fiona asked, not believing it was true but chalking it up to the debts she owed Christie. "Thanks for saving me back there. I'm not sure why Stella seemed…"

"Stella is one of those little officious people who, when given even a smidgeon of authority, goes off on a power trip and runs amok. She kind of reminds me of the cops in charge of evidence. They try to see just how unhelpful they can be."

They had just reached their little corner when a bloodcurdling scream rang out from the other end of the building.

CHRISTIE

*W*hen the scream tore through the happy sounds of an enormous number of authors getting their tables ready and gearing up for what promised to be an exciting signing, Christie wondered if the retired racehorses at Pimlico still thrilled to the sound of the bugle call.

Unlike a lot of authors, Christie was neither shy nor introverted. She loved being surrounded by readers and other authors. But she'd been a homicide detective for far too long not to recognize what sounded like someone having discovered a body. While she'd loved writing her first book and was almost mid-way through the second, the rush didn't compare to that of being first on the scene and bringing a perp to justice.

"Ladies, I think that's my cue," she said with a

grin. "I only have one book so I'm ready to go. Let me go see what that was all about."

She couldn't deny the little thrill that rushed through her. This had a feeling like old times. When she retired after twenty years, she'd convinced herself that she'd left homicide, suspects, and detective work in her past. But gardening hadn't been able to hold her interest, so one night she began writing. Her debut novel, *Prey for Us*, had been an immediate bestseller, catapulting her to the top of the New York Times, Wall Street Journal, and USA Today bestseller lists.

As she made her way to where a crowd was gathering, she hid her smile. *You can take the girl out of the homicide business, but you can't take the detective out of the girl.*

She was busy moving other authors away from whatever happened, using the crowd control techniques she'd been taught on the force. At the end of the hallway was an open door which Christie knew led to a stairwell used by the employees of the event venue. There were several security guards standing around doing nothing, not because they were lazy, but simply because they seemed woefully out of their depth.

"Keep these people back," said Christie, and several guards jumped to do her bidding. "What's happened here?"

The one guard standing on the landing looked like he was going to puke and pointed to the bottom of the staircase. Christie grabbed a small, plastic-lined garbage can and handed it to him.

"If you have to vomit, do it in the trash container. We don't want to contaminate the scene."

Stepping into the stairwell, Christie looked to where the security guard had pointed. Lying crumpled at the foot of the stairs and not moving was Sandy Parkinson, one of the few people who could approach Jessica Murdoch in star or earning power. Where Jessica had been nothing but kind to Christie, Sandy had flat-out called Christie a one-hit wonder on social media and had suggested Christie was nothing more than a flash in the pan.

"Has someone called 9-1-1?" Christie asked the security guard. He shook his head. "Then do it. Keep everyone back and post someone at this door, the door upstairs and the door downstairs—nobody gets in or out."

"Is she dead?"

"I'm pretty damn sure she is. It looks like a broken neck, but I'm going to go down and check for a pulse. Get moving. Time is of the essence, and the cops need us to secure the scene as much as possible. And for god's sake, don't let the readers in here. They'll need to stay in the lobby area."

"What's going on here?" asked Stella as she bustled her way through the crowd.

"Good, Stella, let the event coordinator know we have a possible homicide. She needs to keep the readers in the lobby. The police are being summoned but I don't know what their capacity is for handling this sort of thing. We don't need to make it any harder by letting people mingle…"

"And just who put you in charge?" the short little pixie with the bad attitude asked, drawing her officious self up to challenge Christie with her hands on her hips.

"Twenty years with Baltimore PD—the last fifteen as a homicide detective. Got anyone else you think has better credentials? Or maybe you'd like to go down there and see if Sandy is dead?"

"Um no. I'll go let Lizzie know what happened."

"You do that," Christie said as the little woman hurried off.

"I can do it," offered the guard, who still looked a little green.

"If you want, you can, but I've done this way too many times to count, and it doesn't bother me."

"How come?"

"Because I focus on the body as evidence. Sandy's dead. All I can do to help her or those she leaves behind is to find out if this was deliberate or an accident and who is responsible."

He nodded. "That makes sense. I'm not even sure I'd know how to take her pulse."

Christie smiled at him. "That's okay, I do," she said as she moved carefully down the stairs. One look at the way Sandy was lying confirmed Christie's earlier assumption—Sandy's neck was broken. Christie reached down to confirm the absence of a pulse and found none.

She made her way back up the stairs. "ETA on the cops?" she asked just before she could hear what sounded like no more than two cop cars with sirens approaching.

"Right about now," the guard said with a grin.

"Is Sandy dead?" someone called.

"Someone said she was pushed," called another.

"Folks," Christie said in a reassuring voice that belayed the rush of adrenaline coursing through her veins, "we need to keep speculation at a minimum. The cops are here and will take charge. The best thing we can do for them and for Sandy is to have everyone go back to their tables and give them some time and space to start figuring this out."

The guards started backing people up and dispersing the crowd. Christie glanced down at a discarded tote bag peeking out from one of the tables. Bending down, she could see Sandy's name embroidered on it and a thumb drive peeking out of a side compartment. Knowing she should leave it to the locals, Christie offered up a little prayer for forgiveness as she reached for the thumb drive in the guise of kneeling down to tie her shoe.

Instinct told her to grab the thumb drive and make a copy of it before handing it over to the police. Instinct had saved her ass more than once on the job and she'd rather beg forgiveness later than wait for permission. It wasn't her case; she wasn't on the job anymore, but she wanted to see what was on that thumb drive. Curiosity might have killed the cat, but she'd always been more of a dog person.

Shoving the drive in her pocket, Christie made her way back to her new friends. Something inside her told her these three women were ones she would make lifelong connections with.

"What happened?" asked Fiona, who was really a lovely person and hadn't deserved that snarky bitch Stella's disdain.

"Someone said someone shoved Sandy Parkinson down the stairs and killed her," said Lori excitedly. Lori was the youngest of them and showed great promise as a writer.

"Let's not start speculating. It's the last thing the cops need."

"Do you think we'll be questioned?" asked Jessica, who was cool as a cucumber and most likely had little good to say about Sandy. God knows Sandy had never had anything good to say about Jessica, but then Sandy rarely had anything good to say about anybody.

"Probably. It shouldn't take them long to narrow down the field of suspects, provided they have enough people. We can all alibi each other as we were all down here talking, so we should be free to go."

"What about the signing?" asked Lori.

Jessica patted her hand. "It's most likely over, at least for the day. Christie's right: the cops are going to want to talk to everybody, but we were all together and too far away to have been behind it."

The cops made short work out of identifying those they could let leave the venue and those they wanted to talk to in more depth, although they did caution all of the authors and event staff that they were not to leave the jurisdiction without checking in with them.

"Well, ladies, this wasn't what I expected," said Jessica calmly. "How about if I treat everyone to drinks and dinner at my hotel? The food is excellent, and I don't know about the rest of you, but after what happened to Sandy, I could use a little girl time to unwind and process it all."

They all agreed, and Christie headed back to her own hotel. She wanted a chance to take a look at the thumb drive. Once she knew what was on it, she would know how she wanted to proceed.

LORI

*B*ack at the small, boutique hotel she was staying at, Lori was freaking out just a little. Once she was in her room, she stripped out of her 'serious author' clothes and slipped into leggings and a sweater. While she was sad the signing had been effectively canceled, and even sadder that someone had lost her life, it was the most exciting thing that had ever happened to her.

Teaching middle school biology and chemistry wasn't exactly the stuff dreams had been made of, but she'd been happy enough, hadn't she? Everyone in her hometown had thought her greatest aspiration might be to become a principal, but administration had never interested her. Watching too many of her older colleagues either leaving the profession or burning out had made her question what it was she wanted to do with her life.

When the aunt who had raised her was killed by a drunken driver, she'd left Lori a modest inheritance with the proviso that Lori use it to follow her dream of becoming a novelist. With careful planning and a conservative budget, Lori had asked for a two-year sabbatical. The school district had been reluctant to grant it, but in the end realized they had little choice.

Lori curled up in the window seat of her room, grabbing her notebook and favorite pen and began to make notes—what she'd seen, what she'd heard—all the little details surrounding Sandy Parkinson's murder. By the way Christie acted, Lori was pretty damn sure Christie thought it was murder, and she had spent a long time as a homicide detective.

Unless she was reading things wrong, Sandy's murder had all the earmarks of a great story. While she could jot down her impressions of the scene and what might have happened, Lori realized she needed to get back to the venue to get a clearer picture of the scene. Grabbing her raincoat and big waterproof drover's hat, she headed back to the event site. Even though it was raining, Lori pulled on a big set of sunglasses to further shroud her identity.

She'd run a number of scenarios and tall tales she could tell to get back into the reception hall and was surprised to find the parking lot all but empty. There was no evidence of any police or forensic unit's presence. She parked at the back of the building by the service entrance, taken aback when she tried the employee entrance door and it opened. As the door closed behind her, she had a moment of second-guessing herself. Was it really the brightest thing to do to be wandering around a murder scene just after it happened, especially without anyone else with her? Probably not. She glanced down at the group Jessica had created on each of their phones that would allow them to send a single text that would reach the other three. Lori grinned, the ID read 'Mystery Writer's Murder Club.' She sent them a quick text telling them she'd wanted to take a little look around the scene but would meet them for dinner.

The text messaging notification alarm went off almost instantaneously, but she put her phone away without looking at it. Lori didn't want to be rude, but she didn't want them telling her what she already knew. This was most likely a bad idea, but some of the best adventures she'd had in her life were those that came from really bad ideas.

Walking down the shadowy halls was a bit spookier than she'd thought it might be. She was glad she'd switched to high-top sneakers with their soft and quiet soles. No click-clacking of stiletto heels on the glossy tile floor. She found herself alone in the dark reception area. No sign of anyone else here. With no windows to allow even meager light in, Lori removed her phone from her pocket and turned on the flash-light app to its lowest setting.

She made her way to the far corner of the reception hall where the door to the stairwell was located. She grabbed one of the table maps that she found sitting on the table of one of the other authors. Had the cops moved it there? The tables were still set up as if the event would start in a matter of hours. It was kind of eerie.

Lori reached the stairwell door, which had been propped open, cordoned off with crime scene tape and stepped inside, looking down at the foot of the stairs. Just like in all the police procedurals, someone had used some kind of red dye or chalk to outline the position of the body. It gave Lori goosebumps to see it there and realize that it represented Sandy's last moment on Earth.

But what had prompted Sandy to enter the stairwell in the first place? It was for employee use only and there's no way Sandy could have climbed those cold, hard, cement steps in her Louboutin heels. She had seen them earlier that morning and had a brief moment of envy—she knew what she was wearing. There were windows on the outside wall of the stairwell. Maybe she'd stepped inside for a photo op of some kind.

She needed to talk to people who'd been closer when Sandy had tumbled down the stairs. Had anyone seen someone step out of the stairwell? She wondered if the cop in charge of the investigation might talk to her. She snorted. That was stupid. Why would he talk to her? She was just a writer, and a fiction writer at that. Maybe if she wrote true crime, but she didn't… she wrote cozy mysteries—kind of like Agatha Christie meets Hallmark—no sex, no blood, just well-written whodunits.

Besides, hadn't Christie said that the cops would not want to discuss an ongoing investigation with anyone, least of all someone who'd been there? She really didn't think she or her new friends were actual suspects and the cops had seemed a bit deferential to Christie, but they had pretty much ignored any of the authors who weren't in the proximity of the stairwell at the time of Sandy's death. Lori wrote a note to herself: *what was Sandy's TOD?* Did the other authors in the proximity actually see it happen, or did they just see her body?

Standing at the top of the stairs, Lori felt a shiver run through her body staring at the red outline and knowing a woman had died there not too long ago. She peered over the railing looking, but at what she hadn't a clue. Did she really think there'd be some hint of what had happened? Something the cops had missed? Maybe a big sign that said "The Assistant Did It?"

If there had been anything, the cops or Christie would have seen it, and it would have been removed. She reminded herself she wasn't here to solve the crime; she just wanted to get a feel for the scene so she could use it in a book someday. Isn't that what people said about writers? Everything was grist for the mill.

The empathic part of her demanded that she try to envision the scene as it might have played out. Closing her eyes, she let the scene envelop her. It was as if she could feel the violent emotions swirling all around her—the killer's anger, Sandy's terror. How Sandy had felt as she'd taken that fatal step over the top stair, feeling the malevolence of the person who pushed her and knowing she was about to die. The overriding terror of that moment…

"Excuse me, miss. You want to tell me what the hell you're doing here?"

Lori yelped and felt her ankle give way as she whirled to face her attacker, her arms windmilling around her as she tried to regain her balance. Is this what had happened to Sandy? Had her killer returned to the scene? Was she about to die?

All of this flashed through her mind before the man's hand grasped her wrist, catching her and preventing her from tumbling to her death. Well, if not her death, then at least a nasty injury.

With his other hand, the man flashed a badge and identified himself. "I'm Detective Wilder. I'm going to ask you again, what the hell do you think you're doing here?"

"Um. I'm Lori Sykes. I'm one of the attending authors at the signing."

"And what? You thought you'd come back to get something from your table, or maybe corrupt our crime scene?"

Lori fished out her notebook and pen. "So, you think a crime was committed? Murder?"

"I'm not at liberty to say anything about an ongoing investigation. Why are you snooping around?"

"I wasn't snooping," she said, drawing herself up. "And I'm afraid I can't comment on my writing process, especially when I am developing a story."

That sounded good, not great, but plausible and it beat the hell out of telling him she was here to satisfy her own morbid curiosity.

He nodded. "How about if I put you in cuffs, read you your rights, and you answer my questions downtown in our newly painted interrogation room?"

Lori stepped back and for the second time almost took a nasty fall. Again, the detective prevented it, but this time did not release her until he'd marched her back into the reception hall, closed the door to the stairwell and used more yellow crime scene tape to seal it.

"Um, I really wasn't trying to muck up your investigation. I'm a mystery writer, and I thought I could soak up some ambience for my next book."

"Go soak up whatever it is you need to somewhere other than my crime scene. If I catch you here again, I will arrest you for hindering an investigation. Got it?"

"Yes, sir," she said meekly, turning to leave, walking away, and wondering if he was looking at her butt. He was kind of a hunk. She slowed and looked over her shoulder.

"Out," he ordered, pointing toward the door.

She grinned. Yeah, he'd been looking. With that little bolster to her self-confidence, Lori was off to finish writing her notes. Maybe she'd share what she'd seen and felt with the girls. After all, they were going to form a murder club, right?

JESSICA

*W*ell, the signing today hadn't gone as expected. Jessica kicked off her Jimmy Choo's as she entered her hotel suite. She looked around and smiled. Being a bestselling author had its perks. The suite was truly gorgeous with a separate bedroom and attached bath with an enormous king-size bed, a separate large sitting room with a desk and ergonomic chair, and a bar/kitchen area. There really wasn't a kitchen *per se*, but there was a hidden microwave, a fridge filled with snacks and drinks, and a bar with top-shelf booze. The room was on the top floor and had a panoramic view of the harbor.

The Mystery Writer's Murder Club. Jessica smiled. While waiting for the police to get to them, the four of them had taken the opportunity to sit and talk. They hadn't *networked*, they'd spent time with each other, gotten to know one another, and had begun the process of becoming friends. Jess was pretty sure that those three women were going to play a significant role in her life from now on. Sometimes you just knew when you met someone that you were destined to be friends.

Writers tended to be loners by nature. Being a loner could be a good thing, provided you didn't couple it with being shy or introverted; then, it could make you become a hermit. The fact was that for the most part, writing was a lonely profession. Most people had no clue how people created their works of fiction. Perhaps it was different for those who wrote non-fiction, but at the end of the day, it came down to you and your laptop. As she often did, Jess opened up her laptop and began making notes—observations, feelings, and a brief outline of what had happened.

Afterward, Jessica changed out of the clothes she'd worn to the signing and into something more comfortable—black, leather leggings, a caramel-colored tank top, and a slouchy brown sweater over the top. She pulled on a pair of mid-heeled booties and checked herself in the mirror. She'd learned the hard way to make sure she looked good before going out. Any more she couldn't go hiking with Tracer, her basset hound, without having her hair and makeup done.

Regardless of how scattered, tired, or stressed she might feel on the inside, she realized with a certain amount of fame and fortune came the responsibility to look the part. Sometimes it could be a pain, but every time she didn't take the time to look good, somebody wanted a picture with her. There was always somebody watching, somebody who recognized her and wanted a moment of her time. Seeing as how those same somebodies were responsible for her success, she figured the least she could do was look the part when she went out.

She left her hotel room and made her way to the private elevator, pressing the L for lobby as soon as she got in. Another nice perk of her suite was there were only six rooms on this floor and each of them was assigned an electronic key card that operated the elevator, which meant coming or going there were no stops on other floors.

What a day this had been. She was looking forward to spending time with her new friends in spite of Sandy's murder and the canceled signing. Was it a bad thing to be more upset by the canceled signing than Sandy's murder? Jess didn't want anyone to be dead, but she loved meeting her readers and Sandy had not been a very nice person. The fact was, Jessica could think of a lot of people at the signing who might have had a reason to kill Sandy.

Jessica had already spent part of the afternoon arranging for someone to join her tomorrow morning to help wrap and ship all the pre-orders for her readers. It might seem silly to stay an extra day to get that done, but the idea of lugging all those books back home and finding the supplies to do it herself was just a bit more than she could handle.

The elevator doors opened, and she could see the other three waiting outside the restaurant. She headed across the expanse of marble and fine oriental rugs to join them. From the corner of her eye, she got a glimpse of a tall, gorgeous man who literally dripped authority. He seemed focused on her—almost as if he'd been waiting for her. She steeled herself to be polite, but firm that she wasn't interested. Her most popular romantic suspense series was set in Boston and had not so subtle D/s underpinnings. While it was fun to write about it and her readers seemed to love the alpha males and feisty heroines she wrote about, one too many men had decided she was writing about herself and what she wanted in her own life.

Jessica felt herself relax as he faded into the background without approaching, and she joined her new friends and headed into dinner. The hotel's restaurant was one of the best in the city and its chef had been making the rounds of the celebrity chef cooking competitions where she won more than she lost.

They sat down and gave their order to their waiter. As soon as he left, the four women settled back and began to discuss their industry, offering each other advice and support. They were at four very different stages of their careers, but Jessica was convinced they could help each other.

Fiona looked at Lori and said, "Have you lost your mind? What were you thinking when you went back to the event site? Good god, Lori, you could have been hurt or arrested."

Lori grinned. "I almost was—hurt and arrested, I mean."

"What happened?" asked Jessica, concerned about her new friend.

"I was in the stairwell where it happened…" Christie rolled her eyes and groaned as Lori flashed her a huge smile and continued, "…and this cop startled me. I almost fell down the stairs like poor Sandy and he threatened to arrest me if I came back. Don't get me wrong, I wouldn't mind being handcuffed by the guy, but not fingerprinted and put into a holding cell."

"How do you know he was a cop?" asked Christie.

"He showed me his badge, and he just had that kind of vibe, you know?"

"Poor Sandy," said Jessica.

"I didn't know you two were close," said Fiona, who took a piece of the warm, artisanal bread the waiter set in the center of the table. After slathering it with herbed butter, she took a bite and moaned in pleasure.

"We weren't. In fact, we didn't particularly care for one another. She just always sort of set my teeth on edge."

"I think a lot of people felt that way about her.

She wasn't a nice person, but we don't know it was murder. It could have just been an accident," said Fiona.

Christie shook her head. "I don't think so. I was in that stairwell. The cement had a kind of texture mixed in which would have made it difficult to just slip. The stairs weren't very wide and there were substantial hand railings on both sides. If she'd slipped, I think she would have been able to stop her fall. Instead, she ended up bent and broken at the bottom of the stairs. Obviously, I'm not a medical examiner or forensics expert, but…"

"You think she was pushed," said Jessica.

"I do," said Christie with a nod, "and that makes it murder."

"We should try and solve it," enthused Lori.

Another groan from Christie. "Just what the cops don't need. Four amateur sleuths involving themselves in their murder investigation."

"Well, Jess deemed us the Mystery Writers' Murder Club," said Lori.

"That was a joke," said Jess.

"It doesn't have to be," said Lori. "There are all kinds of unsolved cold cases…"

"Sandy hasn't been dead even twelve hours. I hardly think her murder would be a cold case," Christie said with a little scorn.

"Of course not," said Fiona, catching Lori's enthusiasm. "But we were right there. Christie was the first one on the scene. We might be able to help."

"And we might just be in the way," said Jessica, hoping to add her voice to the side of reason. She could see Lori was enthusiastic and she suspected solving a real murder wouldn't hurt Fiona's flagging career. She and Christie would need to be the ones to curb this notion that they were amateur sleuths and could break the case for the cops.

Christie leaned forward but then sat back as their food was delivered. Leaning forward again, she placed a nondescript thumb drive on the table. "I found this in a tote bag with Sandy's name on it."

Jess stared at the thumb drive as if it was a coiled snake ready to strike. So much for Christie being on the side of keeping their noses out of Sandy's murder.

"Found it?" Jessica asked with a hint of accusation in her voice.

"Well, I saw it and… what can I say, old habits die hard. I picked it up and put it in my pocket. All afternoon I've been telling myself I needed to do a *mea culpa* and turn it in…"

"And yet, here it sits," said Jessica, trying to tamp down her curiosity. It was one thing to joke about trying to solve cold cases; it was another all together to insert themselves in an active murder investigation. Picking up the thumb drive, she looked at Christie. "What's on it?"

Before Christie could answer the question, a

strong, masculine hand reached and plucked the thumb drive from Jessica. "I'll take that. The security cameras showed Ms. Crofton picking up something from outside the stairwell, but we couldn't see what it was. I was hoping she'd bring it with her."

"Hello, Detective Wilder," said Lori, batting her eyes, "it's nice to see you again."

"I thought I was pretty clear that you and your friends needed to stick to writing about murders, not getting involved with one. And honestly, Ms. Crofton, as a veteran of the Baltimore police department, I would have expected better of you."

Jessica snatched the thumb drive back, surprising the detective. "And you should know you can't just seize someone's property. You don't know what this is. I mean, obviously it's a thumb drive, but it could be any thumb drive that Christie picked up anywhere."

"The cameras…"

"You just said they didn't show you what I'd picked up."

The detective nodded. "That's true enough, but it's easy enough to figure it out."

"Is it?" Jessica said, sliding the thumb drive down her cleavage until it was secured between her breasts and her bra.

"Give that back," he said, staring at her boobs.

Jessica knew she had good boobs. Glancing down she said provocatively, "You want it? Come and get it."

. . .

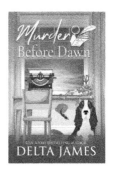

You're invited to join us for the Mystery Writers Murder Club. The first book Murder Before Dawn is available for the preorder price of $2.99.

The only thing more exciting than a famous local author staying at the bed and breakfast is a real murder mystery.

Mystery novelist and member of the Mystery Writer's Murder Club, Jessica Murdoch, heads off for a staycation at a bed and breakfast in her hometown of Badger's Drift, Maine for some rest and relaxation. When a murder takes place in her luxurious suite, she figures it's up to her to uncover the town's secrets and find the killer.

Thorn Wilder, a seasoned detective in the Badger's Drift Police Department, is assigned to investigate the murder. Thorn, an astute and methodical investigator, is familiar with Jessica's work and quickly recognizes her as a potential asset in solving the case. Jessica finds herself irresistibly drawn to the enigmatic detective and becomes an unofficial consultant in the investigation.

Join Jessica Murdoch, Tracer, her faithful basset hound, and Thorn Wilder as they unravel the dark mysteries that lurk beneath the surface of this small town, and discover the shocking truth that lies at the heart of it all.

Murder Before Dawn is the first story in the Mystery, She Wrote series. Four mystery authors meet at a book conference and discover they all live in small towns in Maine. After a fabulous weekend together they decide to form the Mystery Writer's Murder Club. They meet monthly at a different house to check out cold cases in the area, write, and relax. They soon discover the only thing more exciting than a good murder mystery book is an actual murder mystery.

If you like fast-paced mysteries with quirky characters, an inquisitive basset hound, and unexpected twists, you're going to love the Mystery, She Wrote series.

One-Click Murder Before Dawn and get started on your next murder mystery adventure today!

OTHER BOOKS IN THE SERIES

Contemporary Suspense

Mystery, She Wrote (Cozy Mysteries)

ABOUT THE AUTHOR

Other books by Delta James: https://www. deltajames.com/

As a USA Today bestselling romance author, Delta James aims to captivate readers with stories about complex heroines and the dominant alpha males who adore them. For Delta, romance is more than just a love story; it's a journey with challenges and thrills along the way.

After creating a second chapter for herself that was dramatically different than the first, Delta now resides in Florida where she relaxes on warm summer evenings with her loveable pack of basset hounds as they watch the birds, squirrels and lizards. When not crafting fast-paced tales, she enjoys horseback riding, walks on the beach, and white-water rafting.

Delta loves connecting with her readers and tries to respond personally to as many messages as she can! You can find her on Facebook https://www.facebook. com/DeltaJamesAuthor and in her reader group https://www.facebook.com/groups/ 348982795738444.

Printed in Great Britain
by Amazon

32818851R00030